ARGRAFFIAD CYNTAF – 2001

www.y-ddraig-fach.co.uk

Cyhoeddir y fersiwn Cymraeg gan Y Ddraig Fach, sef enw masnachol
Ashley Drake Publishing Ltd
PO Box 733, Caerdydd CF14 2YX

Cyhoeddwyd y gwreiddiol gan Ladybird Books Ltd
27 Wrights Lane, Llundain W8 5TZ

Addasiad Cymraeg gan Dafydd Jones
Argraffwyd yn Yr Eidal gan Ladybird Books Ltd

Mae LADYBIRD a'r logo Buwch Goch Gota
yn nodau masnachol cofrestredig (™) Ladybird Books Ltd.

ⓗ2000 DreamWorks L.L.C.© & ™
Aardman Chicken Run Ltd. a Pathè Image

CYW yn y CAWL

Llyfr y Ffilm

Gyda'r nos ar fferm Tweedy, roedd Ginger yr iâr wedi hen alaru ar fywyd dan gl... yn y cwt ieir, ac wrthi eto'n ceisio dianc. Rhedodd ar draws y buarth mor bell â'r weiren bigog, a thynnu llwy i ddechrau palu. Ymhen ychydig, roedd wedi palu twll yn ddigon mawr iddi wthio trwyddo. Yna, rhoddodd arwydd i bump o'r ieir eraill ei dilyn. Daeth y mwya ohonynt, Bunty, a gwthio'i hun i'r twll – ond fe aeth hi'n sownd! "BRAAAAAC!" sgrechiodd Bunty, "Dwi methu symud!"

Er gwthio a thynnu, doedd dim symud ar Bunty. Gyda hynny, ymddangosodd Mr Tweedy a dal Ginger y tu allan i'r weiren bigog, cydio ynddi a'i thaflu i'r cwt glo, lle treuliodd noson ddu ac unig.

Rhyddhawyd Ginger o'r duwch fore trannoeth mewn pryd i gyfri'r pennau ar y buarth, diolch i ben blaen esgid Mr Tweedy.

"Bore da, Ginger," meddai Babs ddwl. "Sut aeth y gwyliau?"

"Doeddwn i ddim ar wyliau, Babs!" oedd ateb Ginger. "Dwi newydd dreulio'r nos yn y cwt glo!"

"Ond fe gefaist ti amser i ti dy hun," meddai Babs.

Yna daeth y waedd gan Fowler, ceiliog y fferm, ar i bawb sefyll mewn llinell ar gyfer cyfri'r wyau gan Mr a Mrs Tweedy.

Ond doedd un iâr, Edwina, heb ddodwy ers tridiau. Doedd dim byd fedrai'r ieir eraill ei wneud wrth i Mr Tweedy ei harwain i gyfeiriad y gegin. Ar fferm Tweedy, tynged unrhyw iâr nad oedd yn dodwy oedd bod yn ginio Dydd Sul o fewn yr wythnos.

Gwnaeth hyn Ginger yn fwy penderfynol fyth i ddianc. Wedi'r machlud, trefnodd gyfarfod cyfrinachol i drafod cynlluniau newydd.

Yng nghyfarfod y pwyllgor dianc, cyflwynodd Ginger a Mac (prif beiriannydd a dirprwy Ginger) eu cynllun diweddaraf gyda chymorth erfinen. Y bwriad oedd adeiladu catapwlt i'w taflu dros y weiren bigog. Cododd sŵn clwcian nerfus i'r entrychion wrth i'r erfinen daro'r wal a chwalu. Dyma'r cynllun mwyaf dwl eto!

"Wyneba'r gwirionedd, cyw," meddai Bunty. "Does gyda ni ddim gobaith caneri dianc o'r lle 'ma!"

"Ond mae gyda ni obaith cyw iâr!" atebodd Ginger. Sut bynnag, yn dawel fach fe ofnai na wnâi fyth arwain ei chyfeillion i ryddid.

Gadawodd Ginger y cwt yn benisel. "Cyw â'n helpo," meddai.

Yn sydyn, clywodd floedd "Rhyddid!"

Edrychodd i fyny a gweld ceiliog dandi yn saethu drwy'r awyr ac yn disgyn yn domen ar y llawr. Y tu ôl iddo, llusgodd hen boster ffair yn hyrwyddo "Rocky y Ceiliog Handi" – a chododd calon Ginger wrth i gynllun arall godi'i ben.

Rhuthrodd yr ieir â Rocky i'r cwt a rhoi rhwymyn am ei adain, wrth i Ginger esbonio'i syniad – gallai Rocky eu dysgu sut i hedfan! Ond doedd treulio amser ar fferm ieir ddim yn rhan o fwriad Rocky. "Byw ar y lôn – dyna fy steil i," meddai. "Llenwch fy nghwdyn, ac fe ddilyna i 'mhig."

Roedd Rocky ar fin dianc pan ymddangosodd lori o'r syrcas. Roedd y syrcas ar ei ôl! Gyda'i meddwl chwim, gwnaeth Ginger ddêl â Rocky: byddai'r ieir yn ei guddio os fyddai'n eu dysgu sut i hedfan. Doedd gan Rocky ddim dewis ond eu helpu.

Fore trannoeth, cychwynnodd Rocky ar y gwaith o hyfforddi'r ieir. Ond er i bob un ymdrechu'n galed, doedd dim golwg o'r un ohonynt yn codi mwy na phluen oddi ar y llawr ar ôl sawl diwrnod.

"Ymlaciwch, mae pethau'n gwella," meddai Rocky. Ond wrth i Nick a Fetcher, llygod mawr y fferm, chwerthin am ben pob ymdrech a fethai, dechreuodd Ginger ddigalonni gyda Rocky.

Yn y cyfamser, roedd pethau rhyfedd yn digwydd ar y fferm. Cyrhaeddodd crât anferth ar gefn tryc, a dechreuodd Mrs Tweedy fesur maint yr ieir yn lle cyfri'r wyau. Cafodd y dognau bwyd eu dyblu wrth i'r ieir fwyta fel pethau gwyllt. Yna, fe wawriodd ar Ginger. Roedd Mrs Tweedy yn eu pesgi! Roedd dydd y farn ar ddod. Ond pryd?

Roedd gan Rocky ei gynllun ei hun. Penderfynodd fod angen codi ysbryd yr ieir. Addawodd roi'r ŵy nesaf iddo ei ddodwy i'r llygod mawr Nick a Fetcher (doedden nhw ddim yn sylweddoli nad oedd ceiliogod yn dodwy wyau!) ar yr amod eu bod yn dwyn radio ar ei gyfer.

Cyn bo hir, roedd yr ieir yn siglo gyda'r gerddoriaeth, gyda Ginger hyd yn oed yn ymuno â Rocky yn y ddawns. Yna'n sydyn, ynghanol y fflapio ar clwcian, cododd Babs i'r awyr! Hedfanodd am un ennyd fer, ond digon i ailgynnau gobaith yr ieir.

"Fe ddylwn i ymddiheuro," meddai Ginger. "Doeddwn i ddim yn credu dy fod ti'n hidio amdanom ni, ond nawr mae'n amlwg 'mod i wedi camgymryd."

Roedd Rocky ar fin cyfaddef y gwir ynglŷn â'i allu i hedfan, pan gododd stŵr byddarol o gyfeiriad y sgubor.

Roedd Mr a Mrs Tweedy wedi tanio'u peiriant newydd a fyddai'n sicrhau cyn bo' hir fod pob siop yn y wlad yn gwerthu Peis Cyw Iâr Cartref Tweedy!

"Sut mae e'n gweithio?" gofynnodd Mr Tweedy.

"Dyro i mi un o'r ieir ac fe ddangosa' i ti," atebodd Mrs Tweedy.

Cyn iddi allu codi'i chwt, cydiwyd yn Ginger a'i chlymu ar y cludydd i fynd â hi i berfedd y peiriant!

Rhedodd Rocky heb ofn ar ei hôl. Gan neidio i osgoi dannedd y llif a'r llysiau cymysg, gafaelodd yn Ginger a dihangodd y ddau – ond nid cyn iddynt ddifrodi'r peiriant.

Nôl yn y cwt, disgrifiodd Ginger y peiriant peis ofnadwy wrth weddill yr ieir. Cododd ddychryn ymhlith y plu.

"Dwi ddim am fod ar blât cinio Dydd Sul neb!" sgrechiodd Babs. "Dwi ddim yn hoffi grêfi!"

Tawelodd Ginger eu gofid trwy addo y byddai Rocky yn dangos iddynt sut i hedfan. Yfory, byddent yn rhydd!

Yn ddiweddarach, diolchodd Ginger i Rocky am achub ei bywyd. Am yr ail waith, ceisiodd Rocky ddweud ei gyfrinach, ond doedd y geiriau ddim yn dod.

ROCKY
THE
FLYING
CHICKEN SPECTACULAR
IN TOWN
FOR ONE WEEK ONLY
Two Performances
BOOK NOW!
DAILY 4.45 • 7.45 SATURDAY 2.30 • 5.30
GRAND NORTHERN TOUR
Seeing is Believing!
COL. Daniel SPOON'S

Roedd yr ieir yn ysu am weld Rocky yn hedfan. Ond pan aeth Ginger i ddeffro Rocky fore trannoeth, doedd dim i'w weld ond ei hen boster ar y wal. Arno, roedd llun ohono yn cael ei saethu i'r awyr yn y syrcas. Yna gwawriodd ar Ginger nad oedd Rocky yn gallu hedfan o gwbl!

Aeth â'r newyddion drwg at yr ieir eraill. "Dyna ni," meddai. "Yr unig ffordd i adael y lle 'ma yw mewn pecyn Peis Cyw Iâr Cartref Tweedy!"

Yn eu pryder, dechreuodd yr ieir gecru ac ymladd ymhlith ei gilydd. Camodd Fowler i mewn i dawelu'r dyfroedd ac wrth iddo wneud, sylweddolodd Ginger fod Fowler yn gyn aelod o'r Llu Awyr!

Ysbrydolwyd Ginger, a dywedodd wrth bawb am ei chynllun diweddaraf. Byddent yn adeiladu awyren – yn union fel y rhai yr arferai Fowler eu hedfan!

Heb oedi dim, trefnodd yr ieir y cyfan a chyfrannodd pawb at y gwaith. Daeth Nick a Fetcher i roi cymorth wrth ddwyn offer peiriant o dan drwyn Mr Tweedy, yn gyfnewid am wyau oddi wrth Bunty.

Chwyddodd brest Ginger â balchder wrth weld yr ieir mor frwd a llawn egni. Ond ar yr un pryd fe sylweddolodd ei bod hi'n gweld eisiau Rocky.

Yn y cyfamser, nôl ar y lôn, fe sylweddolodd Rocky rhywbeth hefyd. Gallai rhyddid fod yn brofiad unig ar adegau. Aeth heibio i boster anferth yn hysbysebu Peis Cyw Iâr Cartref Tweedy, a dechreuodd Rocky amau ei benderfyniad i droi'i gefn ar Ginger a'r lleill pan oedd ei angen arnynt.

Nôl ar y buarth, sythodd yr ieir mewn ofn wrth i'r peiriant peis ruo i fywyd unwaith eto. Pan ddaeth Mr Tweedy i'w mofyn, gwaeddodd Ginger "Nawr!" a rhuthrodd yr ieir arno. Fe'i glymwyd yn dynn cyn iddynt wthio'u peiriant hedfan i'r llwybr ar y buarth wedi'i oleuo gan oleuadau Nadolig. Daeth yr awr i ddianc!

Ond roedd un broblem: mascot yn y Llu Awyr oedd Fowler, nid peilot. "Dyw'r Llu Awyr ddim yn gadael i gyw ieir lywio awyrennau cymhleth!" esboniodd.

Ond llwyddodd Ginger ei gymell i afael yn y llyw, ac wrth i'r awyren nesau at godi, rhywsut fe gododd Mr Tweedy ar ei draed a rhoi cic i'r awyren. Yna, daeth Mrs Tweedy i'r golwg gan godi bwyell uwchben Ginger. Ond cyn iddi fedru gollwng y fwyell, tarfwyd arni gan sŵn uchel.

Rocky oedd yno, ar gefn beic tair olwyn! Hwyliodd dros y weiren bigog a tharo Mrs Tweedy i'r llawr.

Prysurodd Rocky a Ginger i baratoi'r ffordd, ac wrth i'r awyren godi gafaelodd Rocky a Ginger ar y goleuadau yn llusgo y tu ôl a thynnu eu hunain arni. Roedd Ginger yn dal yn ddig â Rocky am adael, a rhoddodd glatsien iddo. Ond roedd hi hefyd yn falch i'w gael e nôl, a rhoddodd gusan iddo.

Wrth iddi wneud, teimlodd yr awyren yn ysgwyd.
Roedd Mrs Tweedy wedi gafael yn y goleuadau
hefyd! Pwysodd Ginger allan o'r awyren i'w torri'n
rhydd, ond cyn iddi sylweddoli beth oedd yn
digwydd, roedd hi a Mrs Tweedy yn llusgo y tu ôl i'r
awyren yn gafael yn dynn ar y goleuadau!

Ceisiodd Ginger dorri'n rhydd eto pan drawodd
rhywbeth Mrs Tweedy yn ei hwyneb – ŵy! Roedd
Rocky yn ymosod ar Mrs Tweedy gyda chymorth
Nick a Fetcher.

Ond doedd dim digon o wyau! Cododd Mrs Tweedy y fwyell a'i chwifio at Ginger. Dim ond mewn pryd, symudodd Ginger, ac fe dorrodd y fwyell drwy'r goleuadau, ac i lawr fe syrthiodd Mrs Tweedy – lawr trwy do y sgubor ac i mewn i'r peiriant peis!

Cododd yr awyren ac esgyn i'r entrychion.

MIKE

SUPERTED

AND THE
GUN SMUGGLERS

Illustrations by Rob Lee
and Gina Hart

Somewhere on the rocky coastline of West Wales, where the rough moorland stretches down to the cliffs, stands a small cottage. In it, a girl was trying to sleep.

She tossed and turned and then, throwing the blankets aside, got out of bed and went to the window. The moon shimmered on the calm sea. The girl gasped, and felt a tremor of excitement. Out beyond the coast a strange light was flashing!

She quickly pulled on her clothes and ran across the heather towards a small, rocky inlet. Suddenly she stopped. The light had disappeared.

Before she could turn back, a hand reached out from the darkness and pulled her into the shadows.

That year, SuperTed and Spottyman were taking their holidays in West Wales. They lay on a tiny, sheltered beach, enjoying the sunshine.

"Are you coming for a swim, Spotty?" asked SuperTed.

"No, I can never get used to the salty Earth water," replied Spotty," and, besides, it's probably too cold..."

SuperTed did not wait for Spotty. He strode into the water, dived through a wave, and started swimming away from the beach.

He had not swum very far when a large, dark shape passed beneath him and sucked him under the water. His heart raced as the water pounded in his ears, but, with a strong kick, he reached the surface again.

"Bubbling Blancmange! What was that?"

Meanwhile, not very far away, an evil cowboy was pushing the girl down a dark, stone tunnel. It was Texas Pete!

"Get down those steps!"

"Ugh..." Moaned the girl, "it's so dark and smelly!"

"Yeah... I kind of like it myself," said Tex, and he pushed the girl into a tall, underground cavern. Wooden crates were scattered around the edges of the cavern, but in the centre was a pool.

As the girl and Texas Pete stood and watched, a dark shape appeared beneath the water and a submarine broke the surface.

A hatch opened, and two faces poked out. "Coo-ee Tex!"

By now, SuperTed and Spottyman
had left the beach. They were sitting
outside a small country pub,
listening to a coastguard.

"Some very strange things have
been happening," said the
coastguard. "Last night a girl
vanished from her bed. Eerie lights
have been seen in the sea, and
something has been frightening the
fish!"

"Blistering bananas!"

Before they could continue, they
were interrupted by a small boy,
running towards them from the
beach.

"Help!" he shouted. "Quick, I've
just seen a giant, black shark!"

Back in the cave, Texas Pete tied up the girl, while Bulk and Skeleton unloaded the submarine. One by one, they carried wooden crates across a narrow gangplank and placed them on the rocks.

The gangplank was not very strong and when Bulk walked across it, it bounced up and down. Of course, it was not long before Bulk lost his balance and the crate flew out of his hands onto the rocks. The wooden sides of the crate split open to reveal a variety of dangerous explosives!

Bulk picked up a grenade. "What's this?" he asked. "It looks like a pineapple."

"Oh, Bulk," moaned Skeleton. "Please don't. It'll go off!"

It was too late. Bulk had already pulled out the pin.

Meanwhile, SuperTed had said his secret, magic word, and Spotty had strapped on his rocket pack. They flew across the moorland and out over the sea.

"I don't think it was a shark, Spotty," said SuperTed. "I think there's something fishy going on."

"You can't get much more fishy than a shark," said Spottyman, but SuperTed did not reply. They dived down towards the water and plunged into the sea.

At the foot of a cliff, deep beneath the surface of the water, they found the opening to a wide passage.

Boom! Bulk had thrown the grenade into
the pool. The explosion sent water
cascading over everyone, drenching
Skeleton and knocking Texas Pete to the
ground.

"Where's my cigar?" drawled Tex, as he
pulled himself to his feet.

"Here it is," said Bulk, with a chuckle. "It's
burning away in this box of rockets!"

For a second, Tex looked at him in horror.
Then it seemed as if all the fireworks in the
world had gone off. There was a tremendous
roar, as multicoloured rockets bounced off
the rockface and filled the cavern with
dense, coloured smoke.

Texas Pete, Bulk and Skeleton raced
towards the submarine.

"Help! What about me?" yelled the girl.
"Don't leave me here!"

SuperTed and Spottyman were swimming gingerly along the tunnel when the submarine suddenly appeared. It hurtled past, forcing them against the rock wall.

"Oh!" groaned Spotty. "Let's go back, SuperTed."

"No, Spotty," he replied. "There might be somebody in there!"

So they swam on. By the time they reached the cavern the noise was deafening, as rounds of ammunition exploded in their crates.

SuperTed dashed towards the girl and untied her.

"You'll have to be brave and hold your
breath!" said SuperTed.

Then he and Spotty took hold of her and
dived into the water. It seemed only seconds
before they emerged at the other end of the
tunnel. The girl filled her lungs with air and
gasped with relief.

They were just in time. Behind them, the
sea erupted as the underground cavern
collapsed. Rocks tumbled from the cliffs
above them and crashed into the sea.

"You stay here, Spotty," said SuperTed. "I'm going after that submarine."

Leaving Spotty and the girl on a rock that jutted out from the cliff, SuperTed flew low over the water, skimming the tops of the waves until he found what he was looking for; the periscope of a submarine.

He took the periscope in both hands and twisted it around.

Inside the submarine, there was confusion, "Tex, I can't see where we're going!" yelled Bulk. Clang! The submarine collided with a large rock.

As Texas Pete, Bulk and Skeleton rose to the surface, drenched and depressed, SuperTed rounded them up. Their gun-smuggling adventure was over!

Later, SuperTed explained everything to the costguard.

"It wasn't a shark, after all. It was a submarine. Texas Pete used it to smuggle guns and explosives into the country. He kidnapped the girl because she found out what he was doing."

The coastguard smiled and thanked SuperTed and Spottyman. Now the coast would be safe again, for fishermen, for holidaymakers, and even for visitors from the Planet Spot.

MIKE YOUNG

SUPERTED

AT THE BOTTOM
OF THE SEA

Illustrations by Bryan Jones
Chris Kinsey and Andrew Offiler

In his space station SuperTed has a powerful video-scanner which can pick up messages from all over the world.

"Help! Help!" A boy was trying to contact SuperTed from the middle of the ocean.

SuperTed quickly said the secret, magic word and at once changed into the brave superbear. In a flash, he flew out of the space station and down towards the sea.

SuperTed to the rescue!

The signal was coming from a little boat,
full of diving equipment. In the boat was a
boy called Andrew, who looked very upset.

"My two friends went diving for treasure
and haven't come back," said Andrew.

"Don't worry," said SuperTed, with a kind
smile. "Put on your diving equipment and
come with me. We'll find them and bring
them back safely."

He took Andrew's hand, and they dived
into the cool, clear water.

The current was very strong. It swept SuperTed and Andrew towards a beautiful coral reef. Andrew's breathing equipment became entangled in a piece of long coral. He struggled and struggled but could not get free.

SuperTed calmed Andrew and quickly swam away. Then a few seconds later he returned, riding on the back of a swordfish. The helpful fish cut through the coral to allow Andrew to escape.

Soon the current slowed. There, on the bottom of the sea, lay a Spanish galleon. It was covered with sand and seaweed, and long, slimy eels with sharp teeth slithered in and out of the tattered rigging.

Andrew was frightened, but he stayed close to SuperTed and swam nearer to the galleon. He knew they had to find his missing friends.

SuperTed examined the ship carefully. Suddenly he caught sight of a stream of bubbles rising from the other side of the ship.

SuperTed could see the two frightened
faces looking through a narrow crack in the
deck of the ship. They had found the boys.
When they saw SuperTed and Andrew, the
two boys waved frantically and tried to
shout.

"Bu-bubble! Bu-bubble!" Their shouts
spluttered in the water.

SuperTed could see that they were
trapped. With a piece of broken mast he
managed to lever up a plank in the deck of
the ship.

The inside of the ship was full of precious jewels. SuperTed recognised them. They had been stolen from a London museum. But he had no time to look at them now. His first task was to get the boys back safely to their boat.

Just as they were swimming out of the ship a large eel slithered out of the darkness and coiled itself around SuperTed. He spun round at tremendous speed to unwind the eel, and then shook it like a whip. When he let go, the eel wobbled away, looking very frightened.

Once they had reached the boat,
SuperTed asked the boys how they had been
trapped.

"We dived into the ship and found the
jewels," said the boys, "but then someone
bolted down all the hatches and locked us
in."

Before the boys could say any more, a
large black object suddenly rose out of the
water and overturned their boat. It was a
submarine.

A man dressed as a cowboy stood on the deck of the submarine and laughed at them. It was Texas Pete.

"Ha! Ha! Ha! So you got away, did you? Well, you may have found my hide-out but you will never be clever enough to catch me," he said. Then he climbed back into his submarine and sped away.

SuperTed first turned the boat the right way up and helped the boys to climb back in. Then he flew off in pursuit of the submarine.

SuperTed could see the submarine's periscope sticking up out of the water. He flew down and covered it with his paws.

Texas Pete could not see where he was going, and crashed the submarine into a large rock. He rose to the surface inside a huge bubble.

His cowboy clothes were very wet.

When he saw SuperTed, he started kicking and splashing.

"You haven't caught me yet, SuperTed," he yelled. "I'm not afraid of a teddy bear."

SuperTed grabbed him by the arms and pushed him through the water at great speed until he found a friendly octopus. He wrapped Texas Pete in its tentacles, and told the octopus to hold on to him until the police came.

The police were very pleased that SuperTed had caught Texas Pete. They had been looking for him for a long time, but had never suspected that he might be hiding under the sea.

They asked SuperTed and the boys to help their police divers fetch all the stolen jewels up from the Spanish galleon.

Later, SuperTed and the boys took the jewels back to the musuem.

"Thank you very much, SuperTed," said the museum curator. "These jewels are very beautiful. They belong here where everyone can come and see them."

Long queues of people visit the museum every day to look at the jewels. And now on the side of the display case is a little brass plaque which says: Thank you, SuperTed.

Carnival
An imprint of the Children's Division
of the Collins Publishing Group
8 Grafton Street, London W1X 3LA

Published by Carnival 1988

Based on scripts written by
ROBIN LYONS

Cartoon films as seen on BBC and
S4C Television, produced by Siriol
Animation for S4C, the Welsh Fourth Channel

Printed & bound in Great Britain by
PURNELL BOOK PRODUCTION LIMITED
A MEMBER OF BPCC plc

One day, when Ronnie came home from school he rushed into the kitchen to show his Mum a particularly large bit of belly-button fluff.

"Mum, look what I've found," he said, excitedly.

"That's disgusting, Ronnie," she said, but Ronnie just laughed and ran upstairs.

He put his belly-button fluff in a matchbox with some toe-nail clippings and scabs. Then he carefully put the matchbox in a safe place next to the others, his pride and joy collection of over 15,000 bogies, all carefully labelled!

He loved to show off his collections to his family and friends, but they made everyone feel sick. So he was never invited to any parties and he had very few friends.

One day, Ronnie's Dad decided that Ronnie's revolting habits had to stop. "But how?" asked his Mum.

"There's only one thing we can do," he said, "we'll take him to see Uncle Bernie!" Ronnie's Mum turned a very pale green colour.

Ronnie was really excited about going to visit his Uncle Bernie. For some strange reason, he had never been to his house before. Mum and Dad waited in the car as Ronnie ran down the garden path to meet his Uncle. When they saw he was safe, they quickly drove off. "We'll be back at tea time," shouted Dad, as the car pulled away.

"Look at this," said Ronnie, opening a matchbox. He expected his Uncle to be really revolted as he pulled out a big fat maggot. But his Uncle just looked excited.

"I've got one just like it," he said, "come on in and have a look."

Ronnie followed his Uncle inside. "Ugh! What's that awful smell?" he said. "Don't worry about that," said his Uncle. "It's just my pet skunk, Spot."

"I've made us lunch," said Uncle Bernie. "Come into the kitchen. There! Peanut butter, black pudding and banana sandwiches."

Heading towards the sandwiches was Uncle Bernie's maggot collection. A large slug crawled over the digestive biscuits. Ronnie felt queasy and not at all hungry. "I need to use the bathroom," he said. Uncle Bernie pointed up the stairs.

Ronnie had never, in all his life, seen such a disgusting house. He was quite impressed, but, at the same time, he felt a little bit sick. There were smelly socks soaking in the sink. Spot, the skunk, had made his bed in the bathtub and there was a strange, green fungus growing in the toilet. "Now, that is revolting," said Ronnie.

Uncle Bernie offered Ronnie some tea, but he wasn't feeling very thirsty. Ronnie needed a breath of fresh air, so he asked if he could take a look around the garden. "Go ahead," said Uncle Bernie.

But once Ronnie had seen what his Uncle kept in the garden shed he didn't want to play outside.

"Did you enjoy yourself?" asked his Dad on the way home. Ronnie hadn't said much and looked very green. "It was interesting," said Ronnie, "but really revolting."

Ronnie's Mum and Dad smiled at each other, hopefully. "I like Uncle Bernie a lot, but I can't say I'd like to visit him again in a hurry," said Ronnie, "and I've left my pet maggot with him to look after."

Mum and Dad were very pleased. Uncle Bernie seemed to have done the trick after all.

"It's not very nice to be so revolting is it Ronnie?" said Dad as he tucked him into bed that night and leaned to switch off the lamp. Ronnie sighed. "No, I don't think I'm going to be so revolting anymore." His Dad smiled. "I'm pleased to hear that. Now go to sleep, you've got to get up early tomorrow for school".

"Dad?" said Ronnie, before his Dad closed the bedroom door. "Yes Ronnie?". "Can I have a skunk for my birthday?"

Collect all 30 titles in the Little Monsters series

Printed in Scotland by Waddies Print Group. Tel: 01506 419393.